Skeleton Dance

C. JAI FERRY

ISBN: 1-946349-01-1
ISBN-13: 978-1-946349-01-9

Inkwell International
87779 571 Avenue
Laurel, NE 68745

www.inkwellinternational.com

Skeleton Dance

For Lilah

My grandmother wanted to kill me. She didn't tell me this, but I knew it by the way she fed me fried eggs for breakfast every day and conveniently let her foot slip off the brake when I was halfway out the car door at school in the mornings. By the time I was thirteen, I begged to walk to school, which seemed to make her happy. Probably because it would be easier to kill me out in the open, not protected by a seat belt. I once asked my grandmother why she wanted to kill me, but she just laughed her toothless grin and waved me off, telling me I had the same imagination my mother had when she was my age.

My mother died the day I started kindergarten—at least that's what my grandmother told me. All I know is that my mother dropped me off in Mrs. Patterson's classroom that morning and my grandmother picked me up in the afternoon. As we rode home in her station wagon that smelled like dirty feet, she told me that my mother had snorted something up her nose and fried her brain, so I would be living with her from now on. When I started to cry, she reached over and slapped me.

"Your momma ain't worth shedding no tears over. You see me crying?"

She took me to her single-story house filled with dull orange and brown furniture and cigarette smoke and made me an afternoon snack. Fried eggs. I ate two bites before spitting them back up, all over the kitchen floor. My grandmother called me an ungrateful bitch. I asked her why she fried my mother's brains.

The first year of living with my grandmother was filled with screaming matches at home and sad looks at school. Mrs. Patterson felt it was her duty to pat my shoulder repeatedly each day, telling me that sunshine would one day come back into my life. I rolled my eyes at her and told her the sunshine never left. What I really needed was a rainstorm to wash away all the ugly. I rolled my eyes a lot that year. One day, my grandmother smacked me upside the head and said that my eyes were going to stay that way forever if I didn't knock it off. I didn't care. But I stopped rolling my eyes—at least around her.

I should have known that she was trying to kill me when she handed me my Halloween costume during the first grade: an old black gym outfit with thick bands of white paint down the front of the legs and arms.

"Ballerinas wear pink tutus." I stood in front of her, holding up the costume as it spun back and forth on the wire hanger.

She frowned at me from her recliner, her spindly legs sticking up so far in the air I could see all the way up her house dress to her dirty underpants. "You're gonna be a real ballerina, not the fancy kind you see in those dopey books. All skin and bones, like in the real world. See? It twirls just like one of your fancy ballerinas." She laughed, a sort of hacking-spitting-choking sound.

I put it on, determined to prove to her that I would not, in fact, look like a ballerina. As I studied myself in the mirror that hung from the back of the bedroom door, I rolled my eyes once more, then looked through the crack in the door to make sure my grandmother hadn't seen me. I was no ballerina. I stormed back out to plant myself between her and the television once more.

"I look like a skeleton."

She clapped her hands, smiling her toothless grin. "Skeleton, ballerina. It's all the same."

"I won't wear it." I crossed my arms, pushing back the tears when I saw the thick wide bands intertwining across my chest. I told myself to stay strong. I was being stubborn. Stubborn girls don't cry.

My grandmother reached over to release the recliner's footrest, then swung down so she was nose to nose with me. "Then you'll go naked." Her breath made me want to puke, but I refused to back down.

"Fine. Naked it is." I ripped off the costume and threw it at her before stomping back to the bedroom. I was convinced she would cave, that maybe she had the real ballerina costume with its pink tutu hidden in a closet somewhere and would pull it out and say "ta-da!" before swooping me up in a tight embrace and telling me how much she loved me.

Apparently I was spending too much time reading those dopey books.

She didn't pull out a pink tutu or hug me or even let me have the skeleton costume back. Instead, she sent me out into the neighborhood in my pink underwear, shoving an old cloth bag into my hands. She sneered as she said, "Fill it up before you come back."

I refused to cry, telling myself that I wouldn't let my grandmother win. Not this time. I stuck out my chin and decided to collect all the candy I could while vowing that I wouldn't share any with her. Not one tiny bite of chocolate and sugar would go into her toothless cavern.

We lived on a dark cul-de-sac that was full of old people. I was the only kid in the neighborhood, which meant that everyone knew me, but the white-haired wrinkly people all looked the same to me. For the most part, they all smelled the same too, which wasn't a good thing. I started at Mrs. Washington's house next door. She always had a minty smell about her. She also made really good sugar cookies. But her house was completely dark, and no one answered the door when I knocked.

Refusing to give up, I marched to Mr. Johnson's house next. His front porch light wasn't on, which made the walkway dark enough that I faltered. Then I remembered my grandmother's sneer and stormed up the walkway, refusing to look at the shadows chasing me along the way. Mr. Johnson was frowning when he answered the door, and I could tell that he was ready to yell, but when he saw me, rebellious as I stood before him, my hands on my hips and my naked chest thrust out, he paused, then kneeled down to look me in the eye.

"What have we here?"

"Can't you tell? I'm a ballerina." I spun around several times before returning to my chest-thrusting pose. I would not let my grandmother win. Not this time.

"Mmm-hmm, I see." He glanced over my shoulder. "But where's your partner?"

"Partner?"

"Oh, my, yes. All dancers need partners." He raised an eyebrow, as if sharing some well-known fact.

"I…uh…I dance by myself. It's a new dance." I nodded.

"But then who will lift you up into the air?"

I shook my head, suddenly wondering if my grandmother might have been right after all. Could I be a real ballerina without a partner? Mr. Johnson didn't seem to think so. What if nobody else believed me either?

"If you like, I could be your partner." He winked at me and smiled, but it was not a comforting smile. It was a cold smile, a smile that I had seen my mother's boyfriends use before carting her off into the bedroom where they screamed and jumped around on the bed. It was a smile that told me to run, so I did.

I ran straight back to my grandmother's house, trying to ignore her hacking-spitting-choking laugh that followed me into the bedroom. I pulled the covers over my head and finally let the tears come, promising that I would not let me grandmother win next time, no matter what.

Of course it was a promise I couldn't keep.

By third grade I was convinced that I knew my grandmother's game, and I was confident that I could beat her at it. She didn't like it when I questioned her or talked back to her. She wanted me to take her at her word, even when her word changed every day. Lately she'd been complaining about the price of chicken going up. She couldn't eat red meat anymore, because it made her sit in the bathroom for hours until her legs fell asleep and she couldn't get up off the toilet by herself. She'd yell at me to come pull her up. Sometimes I pretended not to hear her.

"If chicken gets too expensive, I'll starve to death," she told me one morning over our breakfast of fried eggs. "I might just stop cooking the eggs and see if I can't hatch a few birds myself. Then we'll have plenty of chicken to eat."

I nodded in agreement, more because I was sick of eating eggs every day than because I wanted to kill and eat a pet chicken. My grandmother always bought whole birds and refused to allow the butcher to cut them up for her. She'd rush home to decimate the bird with the large cleaver that was kept handy on the dish rack. The thought of her getting all giddy about killing my pet chicken made me sick to my stomach, but I shoved the fried eggs in and swallowed anyway.

When I found a dead robin in the backyard, I brought it to my grandmother. I set it on the kitchen table, where she was sitting, reading the obituaries in the newspaper and using a red pen to circle the blurbs of the people she knew. The paper was covered in red.

"What's this?" She set the newspaper aside and clapped her hands. "A birdie—for me?"

My smugness died in my throat. Looking back, I suppose I should have already understood that death did not frighten my grandmother. Instead, she reveled in it, and I had become a willing accomplice in her endeavors. She immediately jumped up and shooed me out of the kitchen. She steered me to her recliner—a place I was never allowed to sit—then turned on the television, flipped through a few channels, and told me to let her know when something good happened.

She returned to the kitchen, leaving me to watch Divorce Court. This wasn't the good Divorce Court of today, where people want to be paid to air their dirty laundry in public. This was the original Divorce Court, which was completely scripted with storylines that made soap operas look like the work of Dostoevsky or Dumas. I snuggled back into the recliner, ignoring the springs poking into my back, and called out tidbits as the actors revealed them. The wife was seeking a divorce from her famous basketball star husband.

"She's a money-loving slut," my grandmother called from the kitchen. "Mark my words. I can smell 'em a mile away."

I frowned. She wasn't even watching the show, couldn't see the pretty lady who was crying as the judge asked her to explain why she wanted a divorce, but my grandmother had already assumed the worst. As the show continued, it became increasingly clear that the wife was truly the victim in the marriage.

"He cheated on her," I yelled out to my grandmother. "Several times."

"So she's a money-loving slut who doesn't know how to keep a man happy in the bedroom." My grandmother poked her head into the living room and gave me her listen-to-me-I'm-telling-you-something-important look. "Don't you ever be like that. Your momma was one of them. Couldn't keep a man happy to save her life. You keep a man happy in the bedroom, no matter what you have to do, and you'll lead a good life."

I flashed a snarky grin. "Did you keep grandpa happy?"

She glared at me and went back into the kitchen. I never met my grandpa. Momma had said he died when she was a baby. I figured they were together in heaven, having a party without me.

I crossed my arms and scowled at the television. I didn't like her saying such things about my mother. It wasn't my mother's fault that she couldn't find a good man. She'd explained to me that there just weren't many left, so she had to find a kind of good one and fix the bad in him to make him even better. She'd tried to help lots of different men. Maybe if my grandmother had helped out it would have been easier for my mother. Maybe then she wouldn't have fried her brain to death. But my grandmother was too busy judging my mother, just like she judged this poor woman on Divorce Court. I couldn't wait for the show to end so I could rub it in my grandmother's face about just how wrong she was.

The show dragged on and on, with nothing new or exciting to share with my grandmother. The wife had been cheated on. The husband made no excuses. He didn't even bother to defend himself. I lost interest when my stomach started growling. The warm earthy smell that reminded me of fresh-baked bread coming from the kitchen didn't help. I felt cocooned in the thought of warm bread, a dollop of butter melting over the fleshy insides. My cheeks flushed in anticipation, and I closed my eyes, imagining myself biting into the warm goodness.

I must have fallen asleep, as suddenly my grandmother was standing next to me, her cleaver in one hand while the other hand was propped on her hip. She was staring at the television and laughing.

"Slut. Told ya, I can smell 'em a mile away."

I struggled to understand. Then I heard the actress on the television program crying, screaming, "He made me do it. He drove me to it." I didn't know what he drove her to do, but I still thought she was the injured the party in the deal. I was about to say so to my grandmother, then thought better of it.

She spun around and headed back into the kitchen, waggling her fingers at me so I would follow her. I sat at the kitchen table, my stomach growling so loudly now that even my grandmother could hear it. She set a steaming crock in the middle of the table, then handed me a plate and fork. She spooned out a generous helping of a dark thick stew-like liquid full of green beans, carrots, potatoes, and corn. On top was a golden crust that gave off the yummy bread smell.

I didn't wait for my grandmother to serve herself before skewering a chunk of potato and popping it in my mouth. The dark liquid was tangy and delicious, and my stomach demanded more. I scooped up forkful after forkful while my grandmother watched. I was too busy relishing in the dish to care. Whatever it was, it wasn't fried eggs or chicken, which made it the most delectable food to ever cross my palate.

It wasn't until the last mouthful that I bit down on something that gave me pause. I pulled out a long hard piece of bone that had an unnatural sharpness at one end. I held it up and looked at my grandmother, who shrugged.

"Them's the breaks when you're eating robin potpie."

I looked at the bone I held between my forefinger and thumb, sadness washing over me before I could stop it. I hadn't killed the robin, but eating it seemed wrong, almost spiteful. Glancing up to my grandmother, I noted the twitch in her mouth, then realized her plate was still clean.

"More chicken for me," she said, cackling as she twirled in a little dance in the tiny kitchen.

I ran to the bathroom before I had to listen to anymore, crying as I gave the robin the proper burial it deserved in our blue-tinted toilet water.

After that, I hated walking to school, but I didn't tell my grandmother that. The birds would chirp as me as I walked, and I could hear it in their voices. They knew what I had done. They knew I had eaten one of them. Each new chirp made me feel sick to my stomach. I never made it to school without vomiting up my breakfast, so I stopped eating in the mornings. My grandmother asked if I was starving myself for a boy. She didn't say the word, but I could see *slut* in her eyes. I would wait until she looked away and then roll my eyes at her. She never caught me. I was learning.

I tried to focus on the squirrels during my morning walks instead, but then I saw one get run over by a teenager racing to school. He laughed in an all too familiar way and backed up to make sure the squirrel was truly dead. I wondered if he might be some long-lost cousin my grandmother never told me about. They had the same cackle, and neither was afraid to use it. That night, I refused to eat dinner just in case the boy had dropped off the freshly smushed squirrel for my grandmother to chop up. I went to bed hungry after my grandmother spent the night giving me the "slut" look. She never said the word though, and I was careful to hide my smile from her. I was winning.

Life with my grandmother became unbearable when I turned thirteen. That was the year I got my period and my grandmother openly and constantly branded me a slut, ranking me up there with every other woman who couldn't keep a man. She took every opportunity to explain that I was not to spread my legs for just any man. I had to find the right man—a good man with a job who wasn't afraid to spend money but was smart enough to keep some for later as well. Each month, when I asked her to buy sanitary napkins, she would lecture me about what being a slut does to a woman, and the only evidence she ever brought up was my mother. It was the only evidence she really needed.

"Don't go spreading your legs if he shoves something up his nose or sticks something in his veins. Those were the ones your momma liked," she told me while we waited in line at the department store. "For them, you keep those knees locked together or you'll fry your brain just like she did."

The cashier was an acne-faced boy I recognized from school. He was a few grades ahead of me, but I didn't care. I offered him a tight smile, an apology for my grandmother. He offered an uncomfortable grin while he bagged the sanitary napkins.

"Are you listening to me?" My grandmother slapped the back of my head. "Quit your ogling. Don't you listen to anything I say? He just wants to take you around back and pull down your panties so he can stick his little boy parts in you. Do you want to be his slut?"

The cashier's eyes widened, and his cheeks flamed red, making his zits glow an unnatural white. I snatched the bag from him and walked out of the store, but my grandmother wasn't finished with me yet. In the car, she reached out and grabbed my knee, surprising me with her grip. Decimating chickens had made her claw-like hands strong.

"Don't be wasting your time on them schoolboys. You find yourself a good man, one that ain't broke, and then you spread them knobby knees of yours as wide as they'll go. You don't like what he does to you? You keep that to yourself. Fake it, just like I've been teaching you to do. Fake it and you'll nab yourself a good man and have a good life. Not like them sluts. Not like your momma."

I wanted to scream at her that I didn't want a man—any man—but I was afraid of what sort of humiliating tirade she would launch into next, complete with a helping of squirrel potpie or roasted puppy dogs. So I kept my mouth shut and faked it, just like she told me.

When the school sent me home in the middle of a Thursday afternoon because I had gotten my period and bled all over my skirt, I was trying to prepare myself for the inevitable lecture. Not that I would listen to anything she said. Not anymore. I'd become damn good at faking it. But I would have to endure her stale cigarette breath and spittle as she raged on.

That lecture never came, though. I found my grandmother in her recliner, her legs kicked up high enough for the whole world to see her dingy grannie panties, the television tuned in to some courtroom drama. I pressed her knees together. Her leftover chicken lunch sat on a plate next to her, almost as cold as she was.

I turned off the television and sat at the kitchen table, savoring the silence for several moments. When the laughter bubbled up, I had the decency to step through the sliding glass doors to the backyard. I would respect the dead, even my grandmother. She didn't deserve it. How many people would circle her obituary in the paper? I didn't know. I would not be one of them.

I waited as the laughter rang out. I would let it have its freedom before shoving it back down and adopting the somber mask that death required in the real world, the world outside my grandmother's house. As I stood there, I looked to the heavens and told my mother that she'd better be prepared to deal with an eternity of hacking coughs and slut shaming. As if in answer, the few clouds in the sky raced to hover over me, and soon the backyard was awash in a spring shower. I stripped off my school uniform and raced naked into the yard, twirling about faster and faster in the rain, holding out my arms and letting the moisture wick away all my hatred and sorrow.

I danced like a five-year-old skeleton ballerina, jumping and spinning, pointing my toes and arching my back while my arms floated on the cool air. All I was missing was my tutu, but I didn't let that stop me. I didn't need the tutu to be a real ballerina.

I splashed through puddles forming in the dirt, then crouched to the ground, scooping up mud to cover my legs and arms. I danced more, pirouetting and twirling, feeling the rain splatter on the mud and menses dripping down my legs. I was breathless, my lungs burning from the exertion, but I refused to let go of this opportunity. I had never felt so pure, so alive, as the day my grandmother choked on a chicken bone and I was finally free to perform my own skeleton dance.

THE EVOLUTION OF "SKELETON DANCE"

I am always writing intriguing phrases and lines that I think should be part of a story on old receipts, napkins, scraps of paper, junk mail—pretty much any surface that my pen's ink can penetrate. The problem is keeping track of all these scraps and then finding the right story for the right line. "Skeleton Dance" is one example where the stars aligned and I found a piece of torn paper with the line "My grandmother is trying to kill me" the day before I participated in a short story writing competition. Although I had scribbled this line more than a year prior, I knew that its story was ready to be written.

Of course, I still didn't know what its story was.

The next day, driving up to the competition, I was unreasonably nervous. This was my first time participating in this particular challenge, where writers were given a theme and then had three hours to write a complete story incorporating that theme. During the hour drive, I was plagued by fears. What if no story came to mind? What if at the end of three hours all I had was a single line? What if the theme was something I didn't understand? What if the story I wrote didn't do the line justice?

And that was the heart of it. That line that I had found while cleaning my office was important to me. It spoke to me in a way I still don't understand. Its story had to be intense. It had to reach off the pages and grab the reader by the collar, screaming in frustration and agony so intense that it would shake the reader to the core. But it also had to have at least the tiniest bit of hope. By the time I arrived at the competition, I had decided that I didn't care what the theme was. I was going to write that line's story (even though I still didn't know what it was). I fully expected to leave three hours later with the start of a story that I would have to write and rewrite and finesse for months to come.

When the facilitator informed us that the theme was "skeleton dance," I felt defeated before I even began. I was sure that this theme was in reference to some cultural event, perhaps Day of the Dead? I could never do it justice if I didn't understand it. Luckily, another participant asked if we could separate the words, use them individually, and we were told we could do whatever we wanted with the theme.

Our three hours started, and I immediately typed "My grandmother is trying to kill me." Then I stopped. Who was this person, and why did she think her grandmother was trying to kill her? I took five minutes to brainstorm ideas. None of them made it into the story, but in the process, I discovered who this little girl was and who her grandmother was.

I started writing.

As I wrote, I imagined my own great-grandmother's basement apartment, and details starting sneaking into the story (I did, in fact, watch my first *Divorce Court* episode while sitting in my great-grandmother's kitchen). Just to be clear, my great-grandmother is nowhere to be found in "Skeleton Dance," and she never wanted to kill me, but her home offered such intense memories for the few times I was able to visit that it brought the story to life for me while writing.

When the facilitator notified us that we had fifteen minutes of writing left, I was typing the last line. I had written a complete story that felt worthy of that first line (albeit I had to tweak that line a bit to fit the story-telling, but I think the line forgives me for that). I walked out to my car and started shaking. Five minutes into my drive home I was sobbing. What had I done? What had I written? I couldn't even remember.

Thankfully, we had been allowed to email a copy of our story to ourselves before leaving the competition. When I got home, I immediately forwarded it to a writer friend whom I respect and asked for feedback. She agreed, put it on her to-do pile, and then life roared into the picture and we all got busy with family, the holidays, and other writing projects. "Skeleton Dance" sat on my computer and waited.

About a month later, I received the news that "Skeleton Dance" (which I had entitled "Surviving Grandmother" at the time) had taken first place in the competition. I'll admit, I got a little squealy on social media about that tidbit of news. My writer friend, remembering she had a copy of the story, pulled it up and read it, then asked if she could create a screenplay of the story. In the craziest twist of fate, "Skeleton

Dance" the short story became *Skeleton Dance* the movie, a noir-style short film created by local filmmakers and actors who produced a visual feast worthy of that single line scribbled on a scrap of paper more than three years ago.

ACKNOWLEDGMENTS

I have so many people to thank for this story, I hope I will be able to remember them all. To Marcella Remund and the Vermillion Literary Project, thank you for providing the inspiration (read: kick in the pants) to get this story out into the world. The short story writing competition took me completely out of my comfort zone, which was a terrifying experience, but now you've created a junkie out of me and I can't wait for the next chance I have to participate.

Lisa Kovanda, Benito Garcia, Kaylie Waite, Rhonda Roth, and everyone else involved in creating *Skeleton Dance*, I not only owe you my gratitude, but I am also awestruck at how you used my words to recreate the visions in my head to such perfection. (And Sabrina Sumsion, I will never forget your giddiness at the film premiere). Thanks also are due to the Prairie Lights Film Festival for hosting the film's world premiere and supporting local talent.

The birds used throughout this story are courtesy of Elizabeth Metz, who (at the time of the writing) was sharing a lot of beautiful, uplifting, and happy bird stories (that of course I had to turn dark and disturbing).

Lynette and Tony Waugh, Adele and John Gallop, Julie Stamps, and Mardra, Marcus, and Quinn

Sikora—among many, many others—have gone above and beyond in supporting this work. My deepest gratitude for seeing something in these words that is worth sharing with the world.

Thank you, Julia Denton, for ensuring that my words make sense.

Finally, I dedicated this book to Lilah Ferry, my great-grandmother, because I truly believe her spirit was guiding me during the writing.

To anyone I forgot to mention, please forgive me. I am no less grateful for your support and contributions, but sometimes my caffeine-fueled brain doesn't always work the way it should.

ALSO BY C. JAI FERRY

Unraveled

Step into a world of struggling fathers, aging English teachers, terrified mothers, plague-bearers, revenge artists, ill-fated lovers, and children searching for their place in life—all characters brought to life in evocative language and imagery that highlights those telling moments when a person's entire life changes from a seemingly simple decision. These bite-sized morsels, most fewer than 100 words, examine the human condition and all its bittersweet moments.

THE HONEYSUCKLE COLLECTION

Honeysuckle Road • Honeysuckle Memories
Honeysuckle Dreams

When I was in first grade, my family lived in an enormous city in the south. My memories of that city are crowded with cars honking and people talking incessantly. I just remember noise. But a few blocks from my house, the river channel was surrounded by honeysuckle bushes, and we would pick the flowers from the bushes and suck on the sweet nectar. It was a haven of calm while the world raged on "out there." Those honeysuckle bushes are long gone, but the feelings they evoked remain with me and often peek through in my writing. The stories in the Honeysuckle series focus on people dealing with some intense emotions as they face changes at the core of who they are. Some rage against the changes being forced on them, others embrace the changes, but somewhere along the way, they have a fleeting moment of detachment, a brief interlude when they too are able to enjoy the honeysuckle nectar.

The Life of Me

A collection of short stories and poetry exploring how perceptions are influenced by our surroundings.

ABOUT THE AUTHOR

C. Jai Ferry grew up in a small rural town in one of those middle states between New York and Los Angeles. She focuses on short stories with narrators who are often described as brutally honest and who likely need some form of professional help. If you've enjoyed this story, please leave a review. Thank you!

Check out all of C. Jai Ferry's novels, short stories, and ebooks as well as free stories and what's coming next by visiting www.cjaiferry.com.

www.ingramcontent.com/pod-product-compliance
Lightning Source LLC
Chambersburg PA
CBHW071230170626
46809CB00005BA/2007